WORLD WATCH
GREENPEACE

Sean Sheehan

Raintree
Chicago, Illinois

WORLDWATCH SERIES

Greenpeace • WWF • Red Cross •
World Health Organization • United Nations • UNICEF

Library of Congress Cataloging-in-Publication Data:

Sheehan, Sean, 1951-
  Greenpeace / Sean Sheehan.
     v. cm. -- (World watch)
Includes bibliographical references and index.
Contents: Greenpeace is born -- The history of Greenpeace -- How
Greenpeace works -- Greenpeace's challenges -- Greenpeace campaigns --
Governments, companies, and the community -- The future.
  ISBN 0-7398-6612-5
  1. Greenpeace International--History--Juvenile literature. 2.
Environmental protection--Juvenile literature. [1. Greenpeace
International. 2. Environmental protection.] I. Title. II. Series:
World watch (Chicago, Ill.)
  TD169.S27 2007
  333.72'06'01--dc21
                          2003001953

Printed in Hong Kong
1 2 3 4 5 6 7 8 9 0 09 08 07 06 05 04

Picture acknowledgments:
Greenpeace cover, 4, 6 (Kezlere), 8 (Beltra), 10, 11, 12, 13, 15, 17 (Morgan), 18, 19, 21, 22, 23, 24, 26, 27, 28 (Sims), 30, 31, 34, 35, 36, 37, 38, 39, 40, 41, 42, 43, 45 (Morgan); Popperfoto 32 (Steve Morgan), 33, 44 (Loren Callahan); Still Pictures 5 (Thomas D. Mangelson), 14 (Hartmut Schwarz), 16 (Pasal Kobeh), 20 (Ray Pfortner).

Cover: Rainbow Warrior, Cherbourg.

CONTENTS

Chapter One:
Greenpeace Is Born

On a calm September afternoon in 1971, an ancient 80-foot fishing boat and its inexperienced crew set out from Vancouver, Canada, into the North Pacific Ocean. The boat was the *Phyllis Cormack*, but it was later renamed *Greenpeace*. The voyage was the beginning of what would become the world's largest environmental action group.

Against nuclear testing

The aim of the trip was to draw the public's attention to United States's plans to explode a nuclear bomb underground on Amchitka Island, a nature reserve in the Aleutian Islands off the coast of Alaska. The crew were Canadians, and this meant that U.S. ships protecting the detonation site could not stop and arrest them in international waters. But the United States government was determined to prevent any interference with the testing of their newest nuclear weapon.

Telling the world

The waters of the North Pacific are often treacherous, and only a couple of the crew had ever been to sea before. For the crew, cameras and radios were their most important equipment. They planned to record the nuclear test and send out pictures and reports to the Canadian and American public. The island stood on an active earthquake belt, and many Americans and Canadians were anxious that the nuclear explosion might trigger an earth tremor.

Greenpeace activist Dave Birmingham raises the sail of the *Phyllis Cormack* during the voyage to Amchitka Island. ▼

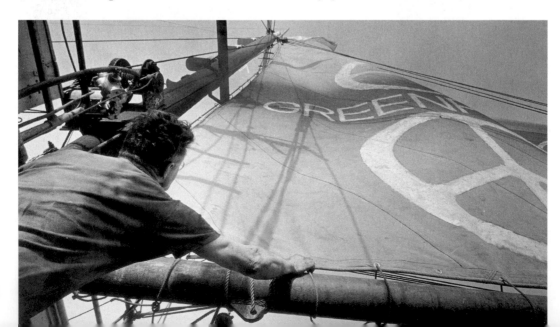

A successful campaign

In the end, the Greenpeace boat didn't make it to Amchitka. Fierce storms forced the crew to shelter in a port elsewhere on the Aleutians. This gave the U.S. Coast Guard an excuse to arrest the crew, on the little-used charge of failing to clear customs. The nuclear test went ahead, but the voyage had attracted enormous media attention and the world was made aware that such tests were taking place. Soon afterwards, the United

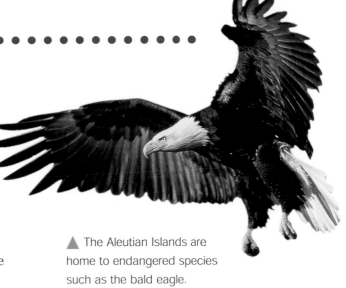

▲ The Aleutian Islands are home to endangered species such as the bald eagle.

States announced that it would no longer be using the Aleutian Islands as a nuclear testing site.

ORGANIZATION IN FOCUS

Founded: 1971

Headquarters: Greenpeace International, Keizersgracht 176, 1016 DW Amsterdam, The Netherlands

Website: www.greenpeace.org

Structure: Greenpeace is a non-governmental organization (NGO)—an organization that does not seek to make a profit and is not connected with any government. It has offices in 39 countries worldwide. The various national offices are run independently of Greenpeace International.

Funding: Financed by contributions from people who join Greenpeace and by donations from members of the public.

Membership: Worldwide there are about 2$^{1}/_{2}$ million individual members.

Greenpeace was founded in a Vancouver church in 1970. It was here that the people who later became the crew of the *Phyllis Cormack* first got together. By sponsoring concerts and asking for donations, the founding members raised the money to hire the *Phyllis Cormack*. At the end of their campaign they had valuable experience in using the media (newspapers, television, and radio) to promote their cause, fundamental skills in taking direct action, and a bank account of $9,000.

The Greenpeace Foundation

Once the group's original objective of stopping nuclear testing in the Aleutians had been achieved, some of the founding members left Greenpeace and moved on to other things. Other members of the original group wanted to keep things going.

They formed the Greenpeace Foundation, with Ben Metcalfe, a radio journalist and experienced Canadian politician, as its head.

Green peace

The protesters chose the name Greenpeace because it seemed to sum up what they were fighting for—"green" because they were trying to protect the environment, and "peace" because they were committed to peaceful protest. Outside of the Canadian group, in countries such as the United States and Great Britain, other groups with similar aims were forming, loosely linking with the Vancouver Greenpeace Foundation.

These are some of Greenpeace's founding members, from left to right Robert Hunter, Patrick Moore, Bob Cummings, Ben Metcalf, and Dave Birmingham. ▼

ORGANIZATION IN FOCUS:
Greenpeace's Primary Aims

The original Greenpeace group wanted to bring public attention to the American use of the Aleutian Islands as a nuclear test site. From this simple aim, Greenpeace's aims have developed to include the following:

- To protect the climate and ozone layer by ensuring that governments of industrialized countries reduce emissions of greenhouse and ozone-depleting gases;
- To prevent overfishing, pollution, and dumping of waste and other hazardous substances into oceans and waterways;
- To change refrigeration and air-conditioning products in order to stop the use of ozone-depleting chemicals;
- To monitor and ensure enforcement of global controls on the international waste trade;
- To protect ancient forests and to promote economic alternatives to intensive logging;
- To eliminate the use of hazardous chemicals—in particular chlorine, which is still regularly used for paper bleaching and other industrial uses in spite of mounting evidence that it is unsafe for humans and animals to be exposed to it;
- To stop commercial whaling;
- To halt the nuclear threat;
- To stop the spread of genetically modified organisms in the natural environment.

Hitting the headlines

Encouraged by their success in halting American nuclear testing in the Aleutians, Greenpeace turned its attention to other areas. France, another nuclear power, was also testing nuclear bombs, this time not under the ground but in the open atmosphere on Moruroa Atoll, part of the French Polynesian Islands in the South Pacific. Greenpeace ships such as the *Vega*, the *Magic Isle,* and *The Boy* sailed out to the test site to try to prevent the tests from taking place. They were harassed by French Navy vessels, and the *Vega* was rammed and damaged.

By 1973 Greenpeace's actions had raised a storm of protest, and both the Australian and New Zealand governments sent their own warships to the area to protest the testing. After Greenpeace protestors were attacked and injured by French commandos, France announced in 1974 that all further nuclear tests would take place underground.

Whales and seals

From nuclear testing Greenpeace turned its attention to whaling and the killing of seals for their fur. In 1975 small Greenpeace boats confronted Russian whaling ships, shielding whales from the harpoon guns. In 1976 Greenpeace began a campaign against the killing of seals in Newfoundland, Canada. The *Rainbow Warrior*, Greenpeace's flagship, was brought into service in 1978 against Norwegian whaling ships, in an effort to get an international ban on whaling.

French navy commandos board a Greenpeace ship near Moruroa in the Pacific Ocean during Greenpeace's protests against French testing of nuclear weapons. ▼

More campaigns

From these early campaigns, Greenpeace went on to highlight the dangers of dumping of nuclear waste, pollution, and other activities that caused damage to the environment. In the 1980s Greenpeace began efforts to protect Antarctica as a world park. By this time, Greenpeace was an international organization with millions of members, and world governments paid attention to its protests.

FACTFILE: Greenpeace Campaigns, 1970s and 1980s

1971 The *Phyllis Cormack* sails to the Aleutian Islands.

1972 United States government abandons nuclear testing in Aleutian Islands.

1973 Crew members of the *Vega* are attacked by French navy commandos in the South Pacific.

1974 France abandons surface nuclear testing.

1975 Greenpeace turns its attention to commercial whaling ships.

1976 Greenpeace launches an expedition to prevent the massacre of hundreds of seal pups in Newfoundland. Active membership of the organization reaches 8,000.

1978 The *Rainbow Warrior* is named and joins the anti-whaling protests.

Greenpeace exposes the dumping of nuclear waste at sea by the British and French governments.

1981 Two new ships, *Sirius* and *Cederlea*, join the Greenpeace fleet.

1982 The International Whaling Commission (IWC) votes, by 25 to seven, to end all commercial whaling within three years.

1985 French secret service agents bomb Greenpeace's ship *Rainbow Warrior* in Auckland, New Zealand.

1987 Iceland announces that it is ending scientific whaling (see p.25).

1988 Sixty-five countries decide to halt all ocean incineration of toxic (poisonous) waste by the end of 1994.

1989 The *MV Greenpeace* succeeds in halting the testing of the U.S. Trident II nuclear missile off the coast of Florida.

Who runs Greenpeace?

By the late 1970s, Greenpeace had offices in the United States, Canada, and Europe. The various offices were linked only by informal ties and this sometimes made coordinating their campaigns and activities difficult. It became obvious that it was time to organize differently.

In 1979 Greenpeace International (GPI) was formed with its headquarters in Holland. The first Executive Director (head) of GPI was David McTaggart, a veteran sailor and campaigner from the 1972 Moruroa campaign, and a successful businessman. GPI's current Executive Director is Dr. Gerd Leipold, who took charge in 2001.

GPI is at the center of a closely-knit network of national and regional offices. The national offices receive donations and contributions from more than 2.5 million supporters. Most national offices then contribute about a fifth of their income to support Greenpeace International and the large fleet of Greenpeace ships.

Greenpeace International and the Greenpeace national offices have an annual meeting to decide which campaigns they should focus on in the next year. Once a campaign has been chosen, it is the job of the GPI campaigns director to decide how it

David McTaggart was the first Director of Greenpeace International. This photo of him was taken on board the yacht *Vega* in 1981, during another protest against French nuclear tests. ▼

should be run. He or she may assign one of GPI's fleet to a particular part of the campaign. National offices have one or two campaigns that are particularly relevant for them, which they work on independently of Greenpeace International. For instance, Greenpeace UK (United Kingdom) is campaigning against the use of polluting incinerators to burn trash, while Greenpeace Canada and Greenpeace USA are fighting to save ancient forests that contain many irreplaceable species of plants and animals.

Once a campaign is under way, Greenpeace International goes into action very much like any international company. The financial coordinator decides how much money

▲ A Greenpeace activist climbs a cooling tower at a nuclear power plant near Koblenz, Germany, in 1993. Activists hung up a large banner reading "shutdown instead of startup." They were protesting plans to reopen the power station, which had been closed since 1988. This dramatic photo was taken from the top of the tower.

the campaign will need, and the personnel office finds the people to work on it. The campaigns director oversees the running of the campaign, and the communications director makes sure that the press and other groups are kept informed about the campaign's progress. Each national organization has a similar group of full-time employees to campaign and raise funds in that country.

Getting money

In the last ten years, Greenpeace has raised its funds almost entirely from money given by the public. In the past, money was raised by street collections and by selling merchandise (things like badges and T-shirts). Today the organization focuses on long-term supporters—people who regularly contribute small amounts of money, rather than making one-time donations. In many countries, such as Britain, Greenpeace is not registered as a charity because charities have to avoid any political activity. In other countries, such as Canada, the government has taken away Greenpeace's charitable status.

Most national Greenpeace organizations not only fund themselves but also contribute to GPI. However, in poorer countries, or countries where a new Greenpeace organization is setting up, GPI provides the funds for the organization.

Greenpeace recruits employees for their skills in such areas as personnel, sales, and communications, as well as for their commitment to the Greenpeace cause. However, most Greenpeace workers are not paid employees but unpaid activists. They take part in campaigns, run the offices, deliver leaflets, and ask the opinions of people on the streets.

In the 1990s Greenpeace membership fell from its peak of over 5 million to about half that figure, probably as part of a general loss of interest in environmental concerns

Rebecca Lerer is a Greenpeace worker in the Greenpeace Amazon office in Manaus, Brazil. Her job is to get Greenpeace stories into local newspapers and on TV and radio. ▶

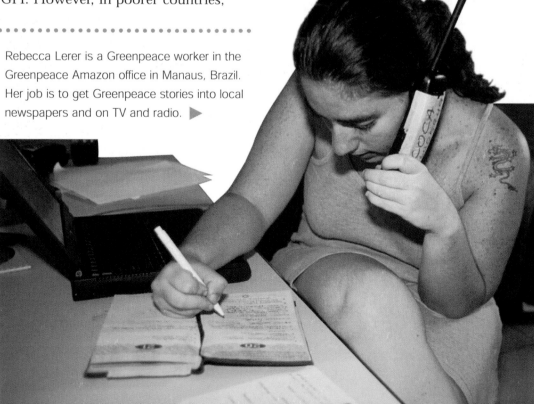

since the mid-1980s. As the number of members fell, Greenpeace's income fell, too.

In recent years the organization has cut spending on administration and has also begun to recruit new members.

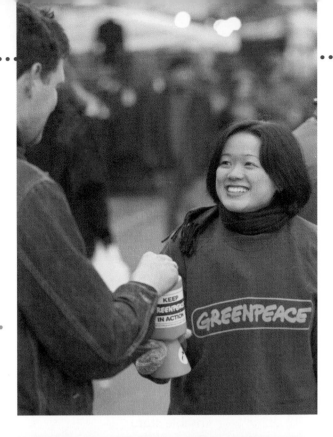

This Greenpeace volunteer is asking for donations. ▶

The global environment

Greenpeace's major campaigns are all concerned with stopping the damage that human beings are doing to the planet. We burn up fossil fuels such as coal and oil, which pollute the air and cause global warming. We cut down ancient forests for their wood and to clear the land, without concern for the thousands of animals and plants that no longer have a place to live.

Not only that, but we dump poisons into the ocean and catch too many fish. We have allowed natural wilderness lands to be mined for profit. We develop new technologies, such as genetically modified crops, without knowing what effects they might have on the natural environment.

Global warming

Global warming is a serious threat to the future of the planet. For centuries, people have been burning fossil fuels such as coal and oil. When they burn, these fuels release carbon dioxide and other gases into the atmosphere. Scientists think that the increased amount of these gases traps more of the sun's heat, which makes the earth heat up. This trapping of heat is known as the greenhouse effect.

As a result of the greenhouse effect, the ice at the North and South Poles has begun to melt, raising sea levels and affecting the world's climate.

Exhaust gases from cars are a major cause of global warming. ▼

The ozone hole

Other gases called CFCs, which were until recently used in aerosols and refrigerators, have also damaged the earth's atmosphere. They have begun to destroy a layer of the earth's atmosphere known as the ozone layer. The ozone layer prevents large amounts of harmful ultraviolet radiation from reaching the earth's surface. Since the ozone layer is damaged, far more ultraviolet radiation can now reach the surface.

Greenpeace's concerns

As we burn the earth's fossil fuels, cut down forests, and dump unwanted poisons into the oceans, we are in danger of destroying the planet's ability to heal itself. Greenpeace campaigns to make governments pass laws to control the damage we are doing to the planet. It also seeks to find other ways of doing things that do not damage the environment.

▲ More than half the world's animal and plant species are found in rain forests. Logging of the rain forest is driving many of these forest species toward extinction.

❝I spent 10 months in Vancouver last year working on the Great Bear Rain Forest campaign. We succeeded in protecting 20 valleys from logging completely and another 68 valleys went into a 2-year moratorium [will not be logged for 2 years]. The coolest thing was when I did a walk with my colleagues into the Elaho Valley not far from Vancouver … I was able to walk through this stunning untouched area knowing that Greenpeace had helped keep it from getting completely destroyed.❞

Tim, a Greenpeace activist

The animal world

Not only is the planet itself threatened by human actions, but so, too, are the other creatures that live on it. Many species have already become extinct, and many more are on international lists of endangered animals, whose numbers are so small that they may soon die out.

Threats to species

The destruction of forests and other habitats on land, and overfishing in the oceans, are two of the main reasons that so many species are threatened. Global warming is also a major threat. It could wipe out whole groups of plants and animals, because living things in a particular environment depend on one another for survival. Plant-eating animals depend on the plants for food, while carnivorous animals feed on the plant-eaters. The plants in their turn depend on insects and other animals to carry pollen from flower to flower, and to carry their seeds to new areas.

▲ These are dead white corals on a reef in the Maldives, south of India. Such damage to coral reefs is caused by global warming.

If one type of animal or plant dies because of climate change, then all the other life forms that depend on it may also die out.

Sea otter collapse

In the Aleutian Islands, where Greenpeace fought its first anti-nuclear campaign, there has been a drastic drop in the number of sea otters. The causes of this drop and its effects show how damage to one species can affect a whole ecosystem. Scientists think that killer whales have been eating the sea otters, because the whales' usual food (sea lions) has almost disappeared. Sea lion numbers dropped because of an increase in the temperature of the Arctic Sea.

The loss of the sea otters has led to an increase in the number of sea urchins, which the otters used to eat.

More than 1,000 species of living things are endangered worldwide. The World Conservation Union is an international organization that maintains a list of endangered plants and animals, known as the red list. Nearly a quarter of all mammal species and 12 percent of all bird species are currently on the red list.

Sea urchins eat a kind of seaweed called kelp that grows in the ocean all around the Aleutians, so as their numbers have increased, the kelp forests have begun to disappear.

Greenpeace campaigns

In the past, Greenpeace has campaigned against the slaughter of seal pups for the fur industry, and against the unnecessary killing of dolphins when they get caught in fishermen's drift nets. Greenpeace has also supported the ban on the trading of ivory and rhino horns, and the killing of endangered animals for their skin or meat. In more recent times, Greenpeace has funded scientific research aimed at proving that global warming, toxic waste dumping, and nuclear energy endanger the planet's species as well as the planet itself.

The skinned remains of this illegally hunted Siberian tiger were found in the far east of Russia. Logging of the forests where Siberian tigers live, and hunting them for their skins, have reduced the population to only about 400 animals. ▼

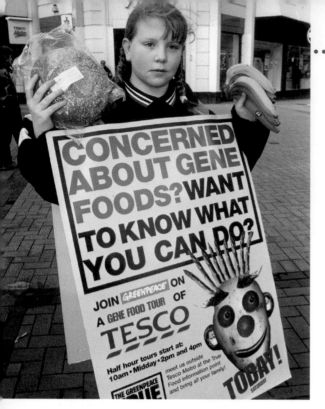

▲ This young protester is demonstrating against genetically modified food outside the "Good Food Show" in London, England.

The human environment

The same processes that threaten the animal world and the planet itself threaten Earth's human population, too. As climate changes begin to affect environments, the people who depend on those environments are affected. In areas of the world such as Africa, changes in climate have brought drought, as the annual rains fail to appear and food crops die. In other parts of the world fierce storms cause major catastrophes. Even in countries with moderate climates such as Britain, changes in winter rainfall have caused minor flooding and damage.

GM foods

Another cause for concern is genetically modified (GM) foods. Scientists have found ways of altering the genetic "blueprint" that decides how an animal or plant will develop. The aim of these alterations is to produce bigger, faster-growing food crops that are resistant to diseases. Some crops have been modified to be resistant to herbicides, which makes it easier to kill invading weeds. However, it is not yet known what the effects of releasing these altered genes into the natural environment might be.

Poisonous wastes

Another threat to human life comes from toxic (poisonous) wastes, such as those from the chemical industry and from nuclear power stations. Toxic chemicals can cause serious diseases in humans, and nuclear waste can cause cancer if it escapes into the environment. Toxic chemicals have been found in animals living in very remote areas such as the Arctic and Antarctic, while recent studies around British nuclear power stations have found high levels of radioactive materials in fish and other creatures in the nearby oceans.

In 1986 the world's worst nuclear disaster occurred when a nuclear reactor exploded at Chernobyl, Ukraine. Today, many years later, there are high levels of cancer among the people of the area. Worse still would be a nuclear war. In 2002 there was a very real threat of nuclear war between India and Pakistan. If such an event were to take place, the clouds of radioactive fallout from nuclear explosions would affect most of the planet.

▲ After the accident at Chernobyl, the damaged nuclear reactor was encased in a huge concrete slab. It is known as the Mausoleum because the dead bodies of workers are still inside.

FACTFILE: The world's nuclear powers

Seven countries are known to have nuclear weapons and have tested them. Israel is known to have nuclear weapons, but has never admitted it or tested them. Iran, Iraq, Libya, and North Korea are thought to be developing nuclear weapons.

Country	No. of missiles	Max. range (miles)	No. of nuclear tests
United States	12,070	8,078	1,030
Russia	8,240	6,835	715
France	510	2,938	not known
China	425	6,835	45
Britain	400	7,456	45
Israel	*100	932	none
India	*60	1,998	5
Pakistan	*10	1,998	2

* Estimate.

CLIMATE CHANGE

Greenpeace believes that global climate change, caused by the greenhouse effect, is the greatest threat to the planet. In 1992 at the Rio de Janeiro Earth Summit, 178 countries met and agreed to reduce the emissions of carbon dioxide and other gases that cause the greenhouse effect. In 1997 at the Kyoto Summit meeting in Japan, world governments agreed on further plans to reduce the amount of carbon dioxide released into the atmosphere.

A small number of scientists argue that the greenhouse effect is natural and that the earth is heating up for reasons that have nothing to do with people or pollution. They argue that countries are wasting money in seeking energy sources that do not produce greenhouse gases, such as solar and wind power, when they could instead spend the money on helping poorer countries cope with climate change. This is an argument favored by industries that depend on fossil fuels. Some of these industries are very powerful and can influence the decisions of governments.

The role of Greenpeace

Greenpeace has campaigned to encourage governments to reduce emissions of carbon dioxide as agreed

◀ This picture shows air pollution from a factory in New York State.

The Greenfreeze refrigerator uses refrigerating gases that do not cause global warming or damage the ozone layer. They are built at this factory in China. ▶

to at the Kyoto Summit. It has already successfully campaigned against CFCs, the compounds that were once used in aerosols and refrigeration systems, but are now banned in many countries because they damage the ozone layer. The gases used in newer refrigerators are less harmful, but they do add to the greenhouse effect.

Greenpeace has therefore worked with companies to develop an environmentally friendly alternative that uses less-harmful gases such as pentane or butane as cooling agents.

Is it effective?

Greenpeace can only campaign, and encourage governments to keep to the terms of the Kyoto treaty. The measures agreed to at Kyoto are seen by Greenpeace supporters and other activists as the minimum that needs to be done to combat global warming. When President George W. Bush announced in 2001 that the United States would not sign the treaty, it was a big blow to the Greenpeace campaign.

FACTFILE: The effects of climate change

According to the United Nations Intergovernmental Panel on Climate Change, it would take an immediate reduction of at least 60 percent in carbon dioxide emissions to stabilize concentrations in the atmosphere at their present level. Making this kind of immediate reduction is impossible but it indicates the kind of pollution cut that's needed to put the brakes on global warming.

◀ These shell-encrusted drums contain nuclear waste. They were tipped into the sea north of the UK between 1950 and 1963.

Nuclear power

Greenpeace has campaigned against nuclear weapons, nuclear power, and nuclear waste since its earliest days. Its long-term goals are to persuade governments to shut down all nuclear power stations and to end all shipments and dumping of nuclear waste. Greenpeace also encourages alternatives to nuclear power plants that are less damaging to the environment, such as wind power.

Nuclear waste

Greenpeace campaigns against transporting nuclear waste, which in the event of an accident could cause radiation contamination of an area. Greenpeace also opposes the reprocessing of nuclear fuel. Reprocessing is a chemical operation that reclaims uranium and plutonium from used nuclear fuel, and turns them into pellets of another nuclear fuel called MOX (mixed oxide fuel).

But the process produces liquid waste contaminated with radioactivity, some of which is pumped into the ocean. There are also worries that the plutonium in the MOX pellets could be used to make nuclear weapons if it fell into the wrong hands.

Such campaigns include the requirements to publicize information on the movement of nuclear waste around the world and across countries. This is so that people will know if a shipment is passing through their area. However, new laws, introduced in Britain after the September 11, 2001 attacks in the United States now limit the information that Greenpeace can publish about the movement of nuclear waste or the safety of nuclear power plants in Britain.

Opposing Star Wars

Greenpeace has also become an important voice in opposing what it sees as a threat to nuclear arms stability caused by the American government's Star Wars technology. This system aims to provide a defensive ring of antimissile systems around the United States so that any incoming nuclear or other missile can be shot down before it reaches its target. It is possible, Greenpeace claims, that if the United States had such a system it would then be under no threat from other nuclear powers and could use its own nuclear weapons without danger of retaliation. In reaction to such a possibility, other nuclear powers may try to make more effective nuclear weapons that could penetrate the Star Wars technology. The hard-won reductions in world nuclear weapons would be lost as another round of nuclear testing and bomb making began.

"Missile Defense was supposed to complete the walls of fortress America. Today, that assumption lies in ruins, and the utter irrelevance of Nuclear Missile Defense to the real threats facing the United States has been demonstrated beyond question."

Anatol Lieven, *The Times*, September 13, 2002

Greenpeace activists outside the headquarters of NATO in Brussels were arrested while protesting against the U.S. Star Wars anti–nuclear missile system. ▼

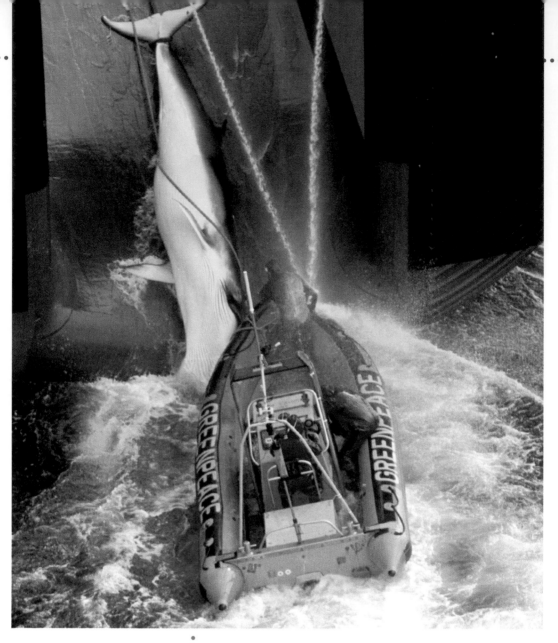

▲ Greenpeace activists try to stop Japanese and Norwegian whaling ships from catching and killing whales. This Greenpeace inflatable is trying to stop a recently caught minke whale from being hauled onto a giant whaling ship.

WHALES

The problem

People have always hunted whales for their valuable oils and flesh. In 1946 fourteen countries involved in whaling, worried by falls in whale numbers, set up the International Whaling Commission (IWC), an organization that aimed to preserve whale stocks. But the IWC was ineffective, and whaling countries killed more and more whales. By 1972 most whale populations were half what they had been in 1946. The United Nations called for a ten-year ban on whaling, but whaling nations were not going to give up so easily.

The role of Greenpeace

In its early days, Greenpeace took on the whaling fleets. Greenpeace vessels followed the fleets in fast inflatable boats, putting themselves between the ships and their prey. Activists filmed the killing of whales and released the films to the media. The actions of a few committed people, working with very limited funds, raised public awareness and prevented the killing of hundreds of whales.

Was Greenpeace effective?

In 1982 the IWC agreed to a moratorium (complete ban) on all whaling, which came into effect in 1986. Greenpeace can claim responsibility for bringing the plight of whales to the world's attention. However, within two years whaling

nations were trying to lift the ban, and every year at the IWC annual meeting, Japan tries to persuade members to reintroduce commercial whaling.

Although whaling has been banned for 17 years, the numbers of some whale species have not recovered as environmentalists hoped. Scientists believe that climate change and overfishing are to blame.

Scientific hunting

Two countries, Japan and Norway, continue to hunt whales for scientific purposes. Greenpeace has campaigned to stop this scientific whaling and for the creation of whale sanctuaries. As well as continuing to take direct action against whalers at sea, Greenpeace also publishes information about whaling to try to persuade people, especially in Japan and Norway, that whaling should be banned. They also take part in the annual meetings of the IWC to fight for permanent protection of whales.

FACTFILE: Whale numbers

	Before mass whaling	1986 moratorium	
Blue whale	250,000	3,000	
Right whale	100,000	10,000	
Humpback whale	200,000	*15,000	
Fin whale	550,000	120,000	
Sei whale	250,000	60,000	
Bowhead whale	30,000	4,000	* Estimate.

▲ Paper mills like this one at Powell River in Canada produce high levels of dioxins.

TOXIC WASTE

The problem

Many synthetic chemicals and materials are now recognized as highly toxic and are a danger to human health and the environment. Some of the most dangerous are dioxins, a group of chemicals that are a by-product of many industries including the manufacture of the plastic PVC (polyvinyl chloride), bleaching of paper, the manufacture of some herbicides and pesticides, and the burning of trash in waste incinerators. Dioxins are present in especially high quantities in major cities.

POPs

Dioxins are the most prominent of a group of chemicals known as POPs (persistent organic pollutants). These chemicals are called persistent because they are not broken down in the environment, rather they accumulate. An international treaty has already been put in place to eliminate these chemicals. Dioxins have been discovered in the stored fat of whales, which inhabit places far away from where POPs are manufactured. They have also been found in people living in the Arctic Circle. The release of dioxins is increasing particularly in developing countries, because companies based in the West have moved many of their factories to countries where workers can be paid less, and lax environmental restrictions exist.

The role of Greenpeace

Greenpeace works to bring the dangers of POPs to the world's attention, exposing businesses that continue to produce these chemicals. They have also campaigned against the use of waste incinerators, which release POPs into the atmosphere. Greenpeace ships measure dioxin levels in harbors and river mouths, where the chemicals have been carried downstream from factories discharging waste into rivers.

Was Greenpeace effective?

Greenpeace and other organizations opposed to the use of POPs have encouraged some big companies, such as Nike, The Body Shop, and Ikea, to eliminate POPs from their products. In May 2001, 91 countries signed a global treaty for the elimination of POPs. This elimination of POPs will

▲ In 2000 Greenpeace activists climbed the world's tallest waste incinerator, Toshima Tower in Tokyo, Japan, to protest the emission of dioxins from incinerators.

not happen overnight, however, and even once their production is stopped, these chemicals will remain in the environment for many years.

FACTFILE: One small fire

Between July 9 and July 12, 1997, at least 440 tons (400 metric tons) of PVC burned in an accidental fire at a plastics factory in Hamilton, Ontario, Canada. The factory was storing bales of PVC material. An analysis of soot and ash samples after the fire at the plant found levels of dioxin 66 times higher than those permitted even for industrial land. This single fire increased the annual dioxin emissions for all of Canada by 4 percent in 1997.

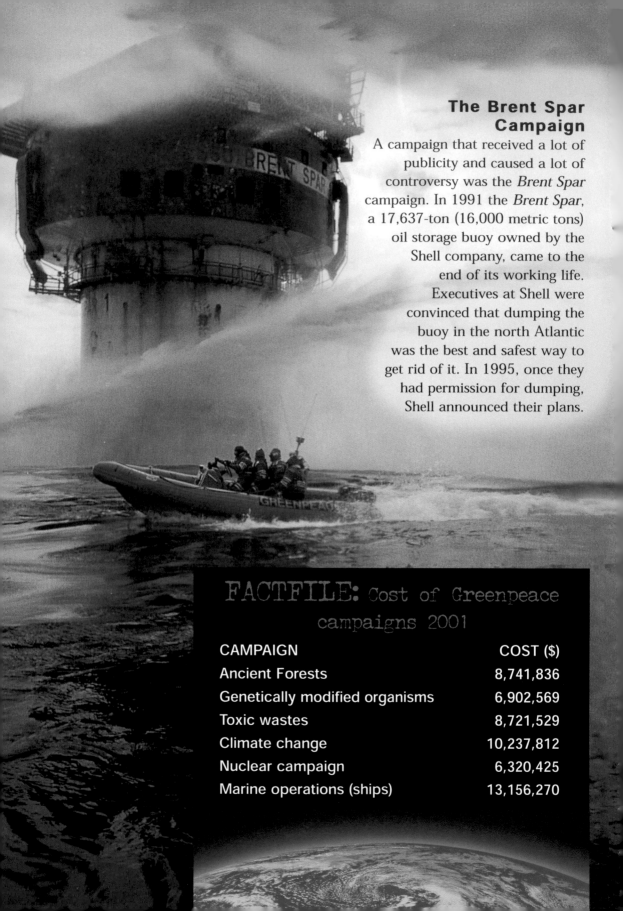

The Brent Spar Campaign

A campaign that received a lot of publicity and caused a lot of controversy was the *Brent Spar* campaign. In 1991 the *Brent Spar*, a 17,637-ton (16,000 metric tons) oil storage buoy owned by the Shell company, came to the end of its working life. Executives at Shell were convinced that dumping the buoy in the north Atlantic was the best and safest way to get rid of it. In 1995, once they had permission for dumping, Shell announced their plans.

FACTFILE: Cost of Greenpeace campaigns 2001

CAMPAIGN	COST ($)
Ancient Forests	8,741,836
Genetically modified organisms	6,902,569
Toxic wastes	8,721,529
Climate change	10,237,812
Nuclear campaign	6,320,425
Marine operations (ships)	13,156,270

Greenpeace and other groups strongly opposed the dumping of the *Brent Spar*. They argued it was wrong to dump huge industrial structures like this at sea, and that industry should recycle and reuse materials where possible. They were also worried that oil and toxic chemicals still in the buoy could cause pollution. They thought that the *Brent Spar* should be disposed of on shore.

Occupying the platform

In April 1995 more than 20 Greenpeace activists occupied the empty platform on the *Brent Spar*. Greenpeace photographers and videographers recorded the occupation, and the Greenpeace vessel the *Moby Dick* stood by to ferry activists and supplies to and from the platform. Shell reacted by removing the protesters from the *Brent Spar*. They then started to tow it to a deep-sea dumping site near Scotland.

During the towing operation, two more Greenpeace protesters were lowered onto the *Brent Spar* from a helicopter. Shell soaked the two new protesters with high-pressure hoses, but they did not leave. In support of the action, many people boycotted (stopped buying) Shell products.

◄ Here, Greenpeace activists try to get close to the *Brent Spar,* but are stopped by high-pressure water sprays.

Success

Greenpeace's campaign received huge publicity and was eventually successful. Shell agreed not to dump the *Brent Spar*, and it was towed into a safe harbor. But when experts examined the rig, they found that there was much less oil in its tanks than Greenpeace had estimated. Greenpeace apologized for overestimating the amount of oil, but said that it was still not acceptable to dump such material in the sea.

A mistaken campaign?

The *Brent Spar* was eventually chopped up for scrap and recycling of reusable materials, part of it being used in the building of a ferry terminal. Greenpeace saw the campaign as a success, since it led to a treaty forbidding the dumping of old oil and gas installations at sea

Some studies done since then have suggested that dumping the *Brent Spar* at sea would have been no worse for the environment than dumping it on land. Also, two marine biologists found that the *Brent Spar* had been home to large colonies of corals, and suggested that leaving such structures in place might be a good way of preserving rare corals.

The campaign cost both Shell and Greenpeace a great deal of money, and some people think it was an expensive mistake.

THE ANTI-FUR CAMPAIGN

The problem

In Arctic areas, seals were an important resource for native people for hundreds of years. They hunted them with simple weapons for their meat, skins, and oil. But in the 20th century, commercial sealing ships began hunting the young animals simply for their fur, clubbing them to death and abandoning the stripped carcasses. By the time Greenpeace began campaigning in 1976, seal numbers had fallen dangerously low.

The role of Greenpeace

Greenpeace activists put themselves between the endangered animals and the huge icebreaking ships that came to hunt the seals. Another tactic was to paint the seal pups' fur with green dye (harmless to the seals), rendering the fur worthless. The campaigns attracted a lot of media attention.

In 1984 Greenpeace launched another anti-hunting campaign, this time against the use of leg-hold traps used extensively in Canada to trap fur-bearing animals.

This campaign was very powerful, using advertising to persuade people not to buy fur coats.

Was Greenpeace effective?

Greenpeace's seal campaign was certainly successful. Worldwide people began to turn against buying sealskin products, and sales slumped. Seal products were no longer fashionable and the commercial sealers no longer had a motive for hunting. In 1982, because of public pressure, the European Parliament banned the import of sealskins. In the Arctic, local people still hunted and sold seal products, but over-hunting of seals had stopped.

Greenpeace's anti-fur campaign also caused sales of furs to slump, but this time Greenpeace abandoned their campaign. The slump in sales had hit the Inuit people of Canada badly. They depended on trapping for their existence and Greenpeace chose the lesser of the two evils, choosing to let the issue go rather than destroy Inuit culture.

◀ This photo for Greenpeace's poster against the fur trade was taken by the internationally famous photographer David Bailey.

"[We] find a seal twenty feet before the monstrous…ice-crushing bow of the *Arctic Endeavour*. We hold our position with our backs to the ship…. The *Arctic Endeavour* plunges forward, picking up speed…. We feel her coming…the ice trembles and cracks. Blocks of chunky ice tumble forwards. The crewman on the ice screams, "Stop 'er captain, the stupid ____ ain't a-moving." The engines cut and reverse. The ship slowly grinds to a halt five feet behind our backs. I pick up the baby whitecoat [seal] and remove it to safety."

Paul Watson, a Greenpeace activist

◀ Paul Watson (left) and Robert Hunter block the path of the icebreaker *Arctic Endeavour* in their attempt to protect seal pups from being killed for their fur.

ANTARCTICA

The problem

Antarctica is a precious, unspoiled area of the world. But it also affects the global climate, because environmental changes in Antarctica cause changes around the world.

There is evidence that there are rich deposits of oil, metals, and other minerals deep under Antarctica. Since the 1950s there have been international agreements to limit scientific and industrial exploration there. But in the 1980s, governments began to discuss exploitation of Antarctica's natural resources.

The role of Greenpeace

It was at this point that Greenpeace became involved, campaigning to protect the continent from the damage this kind of exploitation could cause. Greenpeace began to campaign for Antarctica to be given

▲ In 1997 Greenpeace sailed an icebreaker around James Ross Island near Antarctica. It was only possible to do this because for the first time global warming had melted the ice bridge connecting the island to the Antarctic mainland.

• •

the status of a World Park (a giant nature reserve). It set up a base on James Ross Island, designed to cause as little damage as possible to the Antarctic environment and showing how an Antarctic base could be environmetally friendly.

In 1992, after intense pressure from Greenpeace and other environmental groups, a new international agreement to protect the Antarctic environment was signed. The most important part of the agreement (known as the Madrid Protocol) was a complete ban on mining of the continent for 50 years.

Was Greenpeace effective?

Greenpeace cannot claim that its actions alone brought about the international agreement. But its tactics of drawing attention to what was happening and showing how an Antarctic base could be environmentally friendly, contributed to the signing of the Madrid Protocol.

The purple area in this satellite photo is the hole in the ozone layer. On September 6, 2000 (shown here), the hole covered an area of 10.8 million sq mi (28 million sq km). ▶

FACTFILE: Antarctica

Antarctica is the last great wilderness on Earth. It lies around the South Pole and covers about 5.5 million square miles (14.2 million square kilometers). A mountain range, the Transarctic Mountains, divides it from east to west. It contains about 7 million cubic miles (30 million cubic kilometers) of ice, about 90 percent of the world's total supply of water.

Antarctica has been more affected than anywhere else by damage to the ozone layer. Scientists have found that, at certain times over the past 20 years, the ozone layer over Antarctica has disappeared completely.

In March 1994, the British Antarctic Survey recorded the fastest sustained atmospheric warming in Antarctica since recording began 130 years ago: a rise of 0.9 degrees Farenheit (0.5 degrees Celsius) every year since 1947. Plants that once survived only at the edges of the ice sheets have established themselves further and further south as Antarctica warms up. Along the coastline of the northern Antarctic peninsula, great ice sheets have been breaking up. The most dramatic of these was the Larsen B ice shelf (see page 45).

Some scientists believe that, as Antarctic temperatures rise, the hole in the ozone layer increases due to atmospheric temperature changes.

Greenpeace and governments

During its 30 years of campaigning, Greenpeace has come into conflict with many of the world's governments. Some campaigns have been aimed at governments, condemning certain actions and calling for reform or for new laws and regulations. Other campaigns have targeted international industries such as the nuclear industry, and manufacturers of toxic chemicals or genetically modified crops. These industries are powerful and have a great deal of influence with the

governments of the countries in which they are based. In recent times Greenpeace has taken on the United States government in its anti–Star Wars campaign.

Government attack

In 1985 agents acting on the orders of the French government planted two bombs on the Greenpeace flagship, the *Rainbow Warrior*. When the bombs went off, the ship sank, and one member of the crew, Fernando Pereira, was killed. The *Rainbow Warrior* was in Auckland, on its way to draw media attention to a French nuclear test at Moruroa Atoll. The French government must have been extremely concerned about the threat from Greenpeace to consider

● ●

The sinking of the Greenpeace ship *Rainbow Warrior* ▼

In 2001 the Brazilian government seized these illegally cut mahogany logs, which had been found hidden in the rainforest. Greenpeace worked with Brazilian government officials to stop this illegal logging.

undertaking such an act. The act of sabotage was carried out by secret agents using false passports. They must have thought that they would never be caught. But they were, and the French government finally had to admit what they had done.

Only two of the large team of saboteurs were found guilty of the crime and sentenced to ten years in prison. However, both were free by 1988, less than two years later.

Persuasion and embarrassment

Greenpeace's policies toward governments have become more complex in recent years, involving both the powers of persuasion and the threat of embarrassment. Many of its fleet of ships are equipped with scientific instruments that can measure toxic damage or climate changes. In 2001 the Brazilian government, acting on proof provided by Greenpeace, seized thousands of tons of illegally logged mahogany

wood and banned all trade in the wood. In the same campaign, Greenpeace has taken the British government to court for allowing some of the illegally logged wood to enter British ports.

"For over 30 years, Greenpeace has been at the cutting edge of both environmental policy development and direct action, never losing its radical message. Its role in promoting social and environmental justice is vitally important."

British Parliment Member

◀ The Twingo Smile car, developed by Greenpeace, uses half the fuel of a normal car and has much lower exhaust emissions.

toxic chemicals or illegal logging, Greenpeace invests in developing new technologies, working to produce "greener" products.

Greener cars

For example, Greenpeace has worked with a Swiss company, Esoro, to produce a car with extra-low gas consumption. The car, based on the Renault Twingo, is 176 pounds (80 kilograms) lighter than the original, has less air resistance and a more efficient engine. It produces fewer exhaust fumes, and uses about half the gas of an ordinary car. Some people have criticized the project, saying that the money would have been better spent on developing more efficient public transportation.

An eco-fridge

Greenpeace has also worked with The Body Shop to promote green energy. They have helped put into production in China an eco-friendly refrigerator, using coolants that do not damage the environment. The refrigerator factory provides work for Chinese people and valuable exports for its government.

WORKING WITH COMPANIES

In its early campaigns, Greenpeace's message was usually a simple one: ban nuclear tests, for instance, or stop whaling. But today Greenpeace is much more aware of the complexities of the things it wants to change.

Campaigning on behalf of animals such as seals or elephants, for example, isn't just a question of shaming people into behaving the way Greenpeace wants. Whole communities may depend upon hunting animals, manufacturing chemicals, or using climate-changing fuels. In addition to its media-grabbing events and its work to produce evidence of the dangers of

Corporate offenders

But sometimes Greenpeace still directly condemns the actions of a company or group of companies. A campaign begun in 2001 was the Stop ExxonMobil campaign. Greenpeace believes that ExxonMobil is the oil company with the worst attitude to global warming. ExxonMobil, says Greenpeace, denies that global warming exists and has spent millions of dollars campaigning to stop the United States from signing the Kyoto Protocol to reduce emissions of greenhouse gases. It spends no money on research to find greener alternatives to gas-and diesel-powered vehicles The campaign encourages people not to buy ExxonMobil gas.

▲ In 2001 these windsurfers in north Wales marked the launch of Juice, a pioneering partnership between Greenpeace and NPower to offer clean electricity.

FACTFILE

In October 2002 activists shut down ExxonMobile stations in Manhattan and Beverly Hills. Protestors peacefully chained themselves to gas pumps at both locations and posted a banner that read, "Stop Global Warming, Don't Buy ExxonMobil." The protests marked the start of a national day of action against ExxonMobil by environmental, human rights, and pro-democracy groups.

Community involvement

Within each national organization, local groups conduct their own campaigns on issues that their regional Greenpeace believes it can change. Volunteers sometimes approach people on the street asking for support and giving out information on environmental issues.

Local activists

Greenpeace organizes annual meetings of its local groups to discuss methods and to give training in how to work effectively for what they believe in. Local offices run regular workshops on non-violent direct action, teaching volunteers how to conduct themselves so they do not get hurt. Local activist groups in Britain contribute about $389,000 a year to the organization. One criticism that has been leveled at Greenpeace in the United States is that it has become too centralized, focusing too much on dealing with government and less on the activities of its local branches.

Choosing the right issues

Local groups campaign on global issues such as climate change, renewable energy, genetically modified foods, saving ancient forests, and banning whaling, but they try to highlight ways in which these issues affect local people.

◀ The Irish rock band U2 at a Greenpeace protest in Ireland

In the United States for example, ancient forests are a distant topic to most people, but the fumes from waste incinerators are a clear example of dioxins being released into the air, and every supermarket has genetically modified foods on its shelves. In Canada the fate of the ancient forests is a much more immediate problem, and so local groups focus on that issue.

▲ In 1984 an explosion at a chemical plant in Bhopal, India released toxic chemicals that killed more than 7,000 people. In 2001 Greenpeace activists in Bhopal called on chemical industries to stop producing toxic wastes.

ORGANIZATION IN FOCUS: Fighting the incinerators

In February 2002, Greenpeace volunteers in Britain organized a headline-grabbing campaign against a local incinerator plant. The Onyx combined incinerator and power plant in south London burns over 1,100 tons (1,000 metric tons) of trash a day, collected from homes all over south London. Much of the material collected could be recycled or turned into compost. Instead it is burned in the incinerator, producing poisonous dioxins that are released into the atmosphere. A group of local Greenpeace activists climbed the chimney, closing down operations temporarily. Another group attached themselves to the machine feeding waste into the incinerator, preventing the incinerator from getting fuel. The event brought government policies on waste management onto the front pages of British newspapers.

Young Greenpeace

Greenpeace is not just about climbing tall chimneys or facing down whaling ships. There are many ways in which young people can and do become involved in Greenpeace's campaigns. Children have a right to demand that their future not be threatened by global warming, polluted skies, or dangerous foods.

Young people, like adults, can work for a greener future. Young people are tomorrow's voters, and they can and do write to politicians expressing their concerns. Children can also choose to buy green products, such as sneakers made without producing POPs, or food that has not been genetically modified. They can boycott companies that damage the environment, and they can find out how their own habits harm the environment and learn how to change them.

▲ This Greenpeace solar energy display attracted attention wherever it went.

Young campaigners

Although Greenpeace does not have a youth division, young people regularly take part in campaigns, helping boycott businesses that have been targeted as eco-unfriendly, such as the International Stop ExxonMobil campaign where whole families picketed Exxon and Mobil gas stations around the world. Young people also help raise funds with sponsored walks and runs. In the past Greenpeace has organized a special solar energy bus which traveled around Europe demonstrating to young people how they can have all the conveniences of modern life without harming the environment.

Saving forests

Another important campaign in which young people played an active part was the Kids for Forests campaign. In early 2002 children from seventeen different countries collected signatures for a petition asking world leaders to protect ancient forests. They also reorganized their classrooms to be free from endangered hardwood tree products, produced artwork for public display, and addressed officials of their home countries. Then in April 2002, a thousand children from the same countries marched through the streets of The Hague in the Netherlands, where the International Conference on Biological Diversity was taking place. One young protester said, "We don't want the ministers to just talk...we are here to see that they keep their promises so that there will be forests in our future."

Involving young people

Wherever Greenpeace goes it attracts the attention of young people, who seem to realize that the environment is more important than making a profit. Activists on a Greenpeace ship that went to the Amazon on the Ancient Forests campaign in 2001 spent a day with local children, who explored the ship, practiced their English, and swam with the activists in the Amazon River.

▼ A thousand young people marched through the streets of The Hague in the Netherlands in 2002, as part of the Greenpeace Kids for Forests campaign. Their banners were designed to bring attention to the crisis facing ancient forests.

Chapter Seven:
The Future

● ●

While there are now many organizations dedicated to protecting the environment, none has had as large an effect on the world's media as Greenpeace. In getting its activities widely reported, Greenpeace has been able to reach ordinary people. Its mixture of daredevil stunts, serious campaigning, scientific study, and negotiation with governments and big business, have helped to raise the profile of environmental issues.

Highlighting issues

It may be that much of the progress that has been made on reducing greenhouse gases, protecting endangered species, cutting toxic wastes, and protecting ancient forests would have happened anyway. But Greenpeace has contributed a lot to the progress made.

Over its 30-year history, Greenpeace has found ways to focus attention on issues that governments and businesses would rather keep quiet.

In recent times Greenpeace has focused on a small number of broad issues—global warming, deforestation, toxic products, and clean energy. They have often managed to shame businesses into making their products greener.

Nuclear tests and whales

Some Greenpeace campaigns never seem to come to an end. Greenpeace protests against nuclear testing in the 1980s had some success, but despite the protests, testing continues. In 1995 Greenpeace sent a ship to China

◀ The director of Greenpeace USA's toxics campaign, Damu Smith, addresses a protest against PVC in Baton Rouge, Louisiana. Preventing emissions of toxic chemicals is a major focus of Greenpeace's campaigns.

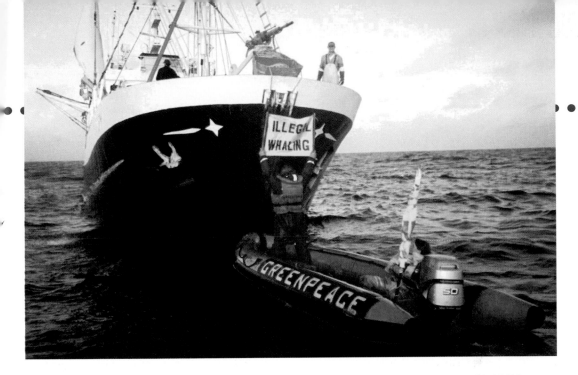

▲ Whaling protests like this one in the North Sea, British Isles, in 1999 have been part of Greenpeace's work since the 1970s.

to protest against nuclear tests there.

In 1996 a treaty banning all nuclear tests was approved by the United Nations, but India has not yet signed the treaty, and in 1998 Greenpeace was once again actively protesting against nuclear tests there.

Whaling is another issue that never seems to go away. In 1985 it seemed as if whaling were about to be restricted, but whalers continue to find loopholes in the agreements that they can exploit.

FACTFILE: Positive changes

In its 30 years, Greenpeace has contributed to many positive changes in environmental matters, from the moratorium on whaling to the control of logging in endangered forests, from establishing Antarctica as a World Park to encouraging big corporations to find green alternatives to their products. Greenpeace has produced an eco-friendlier car, eco-friendly refrigerators, and a solar-powered kitchen. Equally, if not more importantly, Greenpeace has educated generations of people about the needs of the environment and has persuaded governments to modify their environmental policies.

In 1999 thousands of people gathered in Seattle when the World Trade Organization held a conference there. They were concerned about the power of global business corporations.

Facing the future

Greenpeace has changed as an organization over the years. For many of its individual activists, cyberactivism has become an important part of what they do. The Internet provides a forum for discussion on environmental issues and the best way to deal with them. It also gives individual activists a voice. Some have used the Internet to criticize Greenpeace for making compromises with governments.

Internet campaigns have targeted particular governments with e-mail campaigns, spreading information around the world. Activists in different countries can now communicate easily on the issues at hand.

New threats

New threats to the environment, which the early activists had no idea about, have emerged. An example is the Star Wars initiative, which threatens to start a new round of nuclear weapons building. The possibility of terrorist attacks on nuclear shipments, or on reprocessing plants such as Sellafield in Britain, have become much more real since the attacks in the United States on September 11, 2001.

GREENPEACE
AND POLITICIANS

"Increasingly, politics isn't about governments and parties anyway; for many people, it's about corporate power. And while some people may be disillusioned with voting once every four years, many more are getting involved in another kind of politics—taking direct action to stop the corporations."

Laura Yates, Greenpeace

In March 2002, most of the Larsen B ice shelf in the Antarctic dramatically collapsed. Over 1,235 square miles (3,250 square kilometers) of ice broke up into thousands of small pieces. It was one of the most dramatic demonstrations of global warming yet seen. This melting happened faster than scientists had predicted. The main worry is that thicker ice shelves on the colder main part of the continent will collapse, causing a rise in sea levels all around the world.

A worldwide issue

Events such as the collapse of the Larsen B ice shelf bring environmental issues into the public spotlight. In recent years the environment has become an important issue to ordinary people worldwide. Greenpeace has offices in countries such as India, China, and Russia, where the lives of ordinary working people are threatened by pollution, worsening weather conditions, drought, and other environmental problems. More and more, such people are turning to organizations like Greenpeace to find a voice. Greenpeace's future lies in providing a voice for these people.

A huge crack in the Larsen B ice shelf, Antarctica. The breaking up and melting of polar ice is a symptom of global warming. ▶

activist someone who takes action in support of or against a controversial issue

anti-missile systems system of defensive missiles that can be used to shoot down incoming missiles

CFCs (chlorofluorocarbons) chemicals used in refrigerators and aerosols that have been found to damage the Earth's ozone layer

commercial whaling hunting and killing whales for profit

cyberactivism taking action by sending e-mails to protest about issues, or joining Internet newsgroups

direct action protesting about an issue by trying to do something about it directly. Direct action against whaling might involve trying to stop whales from being killed.

drift nets large nets, sometimes tens of miles long that are suspended in the ocean and catch everything that swims into them

ecosystem commmunity of interdependent living things and the environment in which they live

fossil fuels fuels such as coal, oil, and natural gas, which are the remains of ancient plants or animals buried in the earth's crust millions of years ago

genetically modified (GM) food plants or animals in which the genetic blueprint that decides how a living thing will develop has been altered. The alterations aim to produce bigger, faster-growing, or disease-resistant foods.

global warming process by which the earth is gradually becoming warmer, due to an increase in the amount of carbon dioxide and other greenhouse gases in the upper atmosphere

greenhouse gases gases in the upper atmosphere that contribute to global warming

habitat environment in which an animal or plant lives

industrialized countries countries such as the United States that make most of their money from manufacturing and factories rather than farms and mines

international waste trade dumping of toxic waste from industrialized countries in poorer nations. Poor countries are paid large amounts of money to accept such waste.

International Whaling Commission organization set up in 1948 to monitor and control the hunting of whales

Inuit group of native people of the Arctic Circle in North America

Kyoto Protocol part of a 1997 treaty drawn up to regulate and control worldwide emissions of carbon dioxide and other greenhouse gases

National Missile Defense official name for Star Wars, the system of missiles that the United States is building to defend the country against nuclear or chemical missile attack from abroad

ozone-depleting gases or liquids that destroy the ozone layer in the upper atmosphere

ozone layer atmospheric level that protects the earth from harmful ultraviolet rays from the sun

PVC (polyvinyl chloride) plastic used for everyday objects such as toys, window frames, pipes, flooring, and plastic wrap

renewable energy energy that comes from sources that will not run out, such as water, wind, or sunlight

scientific whaling hunting and killing whales in order to study them

synthetic artificial or human-made

toxic waste waste products of chemical processes that are poisonous

ultraviolet radiation radiation with a slightly shorter wavelength than visible light

whaling hunting and killing of whales

FURTHER READING

Brown, Paul. *Greenpeace.* Old Tappan, NJ: Macmillan Publishing, 1999.

Collard, Sneed B. *Acting for Nature: What Young People Around the World Have Done to Protect the Environment.* Berkeley, CA: Heyday Books, 1999.

Morgan, Sally. *Global Warming.* Chicago: Heinemann Library, 2002.

Netzley, Patricia D. *Environmental Groups.* Farmington Hills, MI: Gale Group, 1997.

WEBSITES
www.greenpeace.org
The website of Greenpeace International, which has links to every national Greenpeace organization, a history of Greenpeace, video material, and suggestions for activities

USEFUL ADDRESSES
Greenpeace International
Keizersgracht 176
1016 DW
Amsterdam, The Netherlands
e-mail: receptie@ams.greenpeace.org

Greenpeace USA
702 H Street N.W
Suite 300
Washington, D.C. 20001
Phone: (202) 462-1177
Fax: (202) 462-4507